Limit

Dropsie

Cutie Pie

THE GREAT RACE

Created by Kenn Viselman
Written by Scott Stabile and Catherine Lyon

Published by Jay At Play Publishing

For information please write:
Special Markets Department, Jay At Play Publishing,
295 Fifth Avenue, New York, NY 10016.

ISBN 0-9772256-0-7

Jay At Play Publishing is a trademark of Jay Franco & Sons, Inc.

The Great Race First Printing May 2003
Revised and Reformatted by Jay At Play Publishing October 2005

Visit Li'l Pet Hospital on the World Wide Web at
www.lilpethospital.com

10 9 8 7 6 5 4 3 2 1

Dear Parents:

The most wonderful thing in children's lives is the love they receive from their families. Children derive tremendous pleasure from imitating their parents' care in pretend play and make-believe.

The Li'l Pets in Healy Fields are much like young children in their high spirits, rambunctiousness, and curiosity, as well as in their need to be loved and nurtured. They spend their days playing games, sharing stories, and exploring the world around them. When the adventures are just too much for the Li'l Pets to handle by themselves, the delightful Dr. Foxx is always there to fix their boo-boos and make them feel well and happy again. Then all they need is a li'l extra love from you.

Welcome to the loving and lovable world of the Li'l Pet Hospital!

With all good wishes,

Kenn Viselman

Kenn Viselman

One day Splint the Bunny and Loveblossom the Pony were running together in a field. Loveblossom came to a quick stop.

"Say, what are those red spots all over your fur?" she asked her friend.

Splint held up her paws to see. She _was_ covered in spots!

"Wait a minute," said Splint, looking at Loveblossom. "You've got red spots all over your coat, too!"

Loveblossom stood tall on her back legs and looked at her belly. "You're right," said Loveblossom. "I have even more red spots than you!"

"No," said Splint. "*I* have more than you!"

The two friends hurried to the Li'l Pet Hospital to see Dr. Foxx so that he could be the judge.

Dr. Foxx looked at the Li'l Pets' spots
and spoke.

"Oh, dear, my friends, it's clear to me.
It's poison ivy that I see.

You'll need to stay here. No more play,
Until those red spots go away."

After a bit of complaining,
Loveblossom and Splint settled into
two hospital beds to rest. Their friend
Filo the Lion Cub came to visit them
in their room.

"I'm sure you'll both be better very soon," said Filo.

"I'm sure *my* poison ivy will be gone in no time at all," said Loveblossom.

"I bet *my* poison ivy will be gone before yours," said Splint.

Filo spoke to his competitive friends. "Now you are racing to get well. I remember a time when you two ran a very different race."

Loveblossom and Splint listened to Filo with eager ears.

"Do you remember? It was a beautiful day in Healy Fields," began Filo, "and all the Li'l Pets were gathered together with excitement."

Some held signs that said, "Go,

Loveblossom!" Some held signs
that said, "Go, Splint!"

It was the day of the great race.
Loveblossom and Splint closed their
eyes and remembered.

They were going to see who was the
fastest pet in Healy Fields. They stood
at the starting line, which was marked
by the root of a giant elm tree.

Their friend Cutie Pie the Giraffe held
her scarf up in the air. "When my
scarf hits the ground," she yelled, "let
the race begin!"

"Ready . . . . One . . . two . . ." But just as Cutie Pie was about to release her scarf, a big gust of wind carried it off. "Oh, no!" said Cutie Pie. "My favorite scarf is blowing away!"

"Don't worry, Cutie Pie, I'll get it,"
said both Loveblossom and Splint at
the same time.

"No, I'll get it," said Loveblossom.

"No, I'll get it," said Splint.
The two friends sprinted after the

scarf. Loveblossom galloped as fast as
she could. She nearly caught the scarf
in her teeth, but the wind carried it
just out of her reach.

Splint hopped high toward the scarf. She nearly caught it in her paws, but the wind carried it just out of her reach, too.

The two racers kept galloping and hopping back and forth all through Healy Fields, but the wind was too strong. The scarf kept flying away.

The rest of their friends were much slower and could not keep up.

Finally, the wind stopped blowing and Cutie Pie's scarf floated to the ground.

Loveblossom and Splint were terribly
tired from all their running and
hopping. They walked slowly over
to the scarf and settled down on the
ground beside it.

Soon their friends caught up with them.

"Okay," said Cutie Pie. "Now that I've got my favorite scarf back, let's start the race!"

"Go, Splint, go!" yelled Stomp the Elephant and Dropsie the Bear Cub.

"Go, Loveblossom, go!" yelled Scuffs
the Kitten and Limit the Puppy.

"I want you both to win!" yelled
loyal Filo.

Loveblossom looked up at her friends. "I think I'll have to win the race another day," she said.

Splint looked up at her friends. "I think I'll have to win the race another day, too," she said.

The two buddies snuggled together and fell fast asleep.

"And that's the story of the great race," Filo said, finishing his story.

He looked at his friends in their
hospital beds. Once again, Loveblossom
and Splint were fast asleep. Filo pulled
up their covers, turned out the light,
and tiptoed out of the room.

And now... All they need

li'l extra love from you!

Dr. Foxx says:

It's okay to challenge a friend.
You all are winners in the end.

Just be careful, check the ground.
Make sure there isn't poison ivy around.

Now give your pet a hug and kisses,
And go for a walk wherever she wishes.